D1232618

What a Life!

What a Life!

AN AUTOBIOGRAPHY

BY

E. V. Lucas

AND

George Morrow

ILLUSTRATED BY WHITELEY'S

WITH A NEW INTRODUCTION BY

JOHN ASHBERY

DOVER PUBLICATIONS, INC., NEW YORK

International Standard Book Number: 0-486-23133-X
Library of Congress Catalog Card Number: 74-16979

Manufactured in the United States of America
Dover Publications, Inc.
180 Varick Street
New York, N.Y. 10014

INTRODUCTION
TO THE DOVER EDITION

In a volume of literary reminiscences called *Reading, Writing and Remembering,* published in 1932, Edward Verrall Lucas gives the following account of the composition of *What a Life!*:

"In 1911 George Morrow and I hit upon the device of forcing the blocks in a stores catalogue to illustrate a biography, and produced *What a Life! . . .* We applied first to Harrod's for permission and, being refused, went to Whiteley's and were made welcome. The next thing was to get scissors and paste and let ourselves go; and the process of bending the material to our will was, I can assure you, very exhilarating.

"The book had very little popularity, but it won a few very faithful friends, and I know one house where a copy of it is chained to the side of the mantelpiece like a Bible in church.

"A year or so ago it formed the basis of a lantern lecture at the Grafton Theatre, the arranged fee for which has not yet been paid.

"It would be amusing to give the joke a second chance, but the illustrated shilling book is dead, killed by the rise in the prices of production which set in during the War; and to ask more than a shilling would be foolish."

Here one may take issue with Mr. Lucas, who is not the first man of letters to underestimate his lighter productions. The illustrated shilling book is gone, but *What a Life!* is very much alive. The object of a small but enthusiastic cult, it has become a collector's item and certainly deserves to be reprinted at the present going rate. In fact this tiny classic of proto-Dada seems likely to outlive all of Lucas' other books (more than sixty altogether, with titles like *A Wanderer in Paris* and *Roving East and Roving West*), if indeed anybody still reads them.

What a Life! is a very funny book and deserves a niche in the pantheon of British nonsense. It also has a certain place in the history of modern art, predating by almost a decade the collages of Max Ernst, who also drew inspiration (but for very different ends) from the engravings in illustrated catalogues. The fact has been noted by Herta Wescher in her monumental history of the medium entitled *Collage*. And Raymond Queneau, the French novelist and former member of the Surrealist group, has a brief essay on *What a Life!* in his book *Bâtons, Chiffres et Lettres,* citing its publication date (August 17, 1911) as the moment of the first conjunction of scissors and glue-pot "with disinterested ends in view." The book's importance as an object of fantastic art was consecrated in the 1936 Museum of Modern Art exhibition "Fantastic Art, Dada and Surrealism," where two of its illustrations were included at the suggestion of the writer Jay Leyda, who was at that time on the Museum's staff and had discovered *What a Life!* in a London bookshop a few years before.

Although there is no evidence that Max Ernst knew Lucas' and Morrow's little book, the resemblances between it and such a work as Ernst's collage novel *Une Semaine de Bonté* are striking. Of course the raw material—those old steel engravings—was already charged with disturbing suggestions, waiting to be incorporated into fantasy. Queneau mentions the "memory of the precise uneasiness" produced by the catalogues his mother received from the Grande Maison de Blanc. And Marcel Jean in his *History of Surrealist Painting* has noted that at the time when Ernst first began cutting up steel-engraved illustrations, this method of reproduction was already old-fashioned and evocative of childhood memories for the people of his generation: "possessing a picturesque quality that is both derisive and very engaging, and which becomes enhanced, revivified by the very humor of the collage." Yet there is terror in Ernst's collages, for example in the "Cour du Dragon" sequence of *Une Semaine de Bonté,* where an already turbulent *drame bourgeois* is complicated by the bat's wings and reptilian members that its elegant characters keep sprouting. The terror is heightened by the fact that these figures who once stood as symbols of taste and correctness have changed character and are now rampaging in a world of nightmare.

There is no terror in *What a Life!*, but there are veiled suggestions of the *trouble* mentioned by Queneau, and it is present not only in such gothic touches as the "headless apparition" of Sir Easton West's Tudor manor and the bloody handprint that figured in the stolen diamonds case at Closure Castle. It can be felt throughout in the dislocations, sometimes farcically broad but sometimes very slight, that separate the pictures from the text.

Marcel Jean says of Ernst's collages that "his point of departure is literally a cliché." Lucas' and Morrow's work is even more deeply rooted in the cliché: in addition to the cliché reproductions of visual stereotypes from Whiteley's catalogue, the story itself is a continuous literary cliché, deftly sabotaged on every page by the authors' finely honed scissors and pen. Here as usual the satirist's attitude toward his material is ambivalent—a "love-hate relationship." Lucas was precisely a writer "entrapped by teatime fame and by commuters' comforts," in Marianne Moore's phrase. He wrote compulsively and continually, using the proceeds to live well in the manner suggested by the frock-coated gentlemen and aigretted ladies who stare from the pages of Whiteley's catalogue, surrounded by those solemn and superfluous luxury goods which sometimes seem so essential to life. Yet he is constantly ridiculing the upper classes or rather the ambition to belong to them which the catalogue meant to insinuate into its readers.

The visual satire is effected through various techniques. One is the collaged juxtaposition of incongru-

ously unrelated objects (in the manner of Lautréamont's
famous "fortuitous encounter of an umbrella and a
sewing machine on a dissecting table"). There are rela-
tively few examples of this kind of pre-Surrealist collage
in *What a Life!* One of them depicts the unfortunate
Lady Goosepelt, a chronic invalid who lived at Bournemouth "in a charming villegiatura." But the illustration
shows a horsedrawn trash can from which emerges, as in
Beckett's *Endgame,* the head of a lady of quality wearing
an ostrich-trimmed hat. Another example is the picture
of Lord Crewett, "who was never out of riding breeches,"
and whose breeches are in fact a pair of inverted cruets.
But the authors' usual method is to present a single image
from the catalogue, diverted from its original context by
the accompanying caption. Sometimes the text ridicules
the very crudeness of the reproduction, as in the illustration of Lady Goosepelt's eccentric husband Sir William,
a figure standing under a shower from which heavy lines
of water issue, with the legend: "Among his other odd
ways he often indulged in the luxury of a treacle bath."
Throughout it is the proliferation of consumer goods
deemed indispensable to the well-stocked Edwardian
household that is under attack. An elaborate jellied
prawn salad turned out of a mold from Whiteley's becomes a new hat sent down from London for the narrator's bride; on the same page a hideous scrollwork
bonheur-du-jour laden with gewgaws is billed as his
"unique collection of Sèvres." The occasional moments
of a slightly darker humor such as the headless appari-

tion (actually a dress on a hanger emerging from a steamer trunk) and the Paticaka railway disaster are strikingly premonitory of Ernst's *La Femme 100 Têtes* (a pun on "La Femme sans Tête") . Yet, in the absence of any known link one must assume that Lucas and Ernst were simply in touch with the same Zeitgeist and received emanations of the same absurdity through the medium of a popular imagery, although what in Lucas' work are only polite suggestions of anarchy have become destructive paroxysms in Ernst's.

This bit of "shilling nonsense" as Lucas called it was but one of a number of collaborations between him and George Morrow. The latter, born in Belfast in 1869, was a popular illustrator and a regular contributor to *Punch* from 1906 almost to his death in 1955. Morrow's style is neat, fluent and idiomatic without any obvious tics; it is somewhat reminiscent of the French caricaturist Caran d'Ache whose work was popular in France at the time Morrow was a student there. It seems likely that the crisp *mise en page* of *What a Life!* was more Morrow's creation than Lucas', though both probably collaborated on the "plot" and the jokes; like Lucas, Morrow had a reputation as a wit.

Lucas' daughter Audrey left a memoir of her father which tells us very little about him (though considerably more than Lucas' own volumes of "reminiscences"). We learn from her that he was rather irritable, hated draughts and believed in the importance of masticating bread with one's meals. Somehow he himself sounds a likely tenant of Frisby Towers, the cardboard castle where the narrator of *What a Life!* finally settles with his bride ("We were idyllically happy at Frisby Towers, in spite of its outward air of gloom"). An anecdote Audrey Lucas tells of Lucas' later years (he died in 1938 at the age of seventy), after he had left his family for an undivulged reason and set up housekeeping on his own, suggests that he may finally have ended up living out the fantasies he had pilloried so wittily years before. "He did, I suppose, go in for a good many of the frills of life; but at these he was quite able to laugh, almost to sneer even. Part of his house in the country had been converted from a cottage, occupied many years before by a shepherd; and E. V., telling me one day that his dining-room, which had in it a great open fireplace, and had been in the shepherd's time the kitchen, went on to say, 'Sometimes when I'm having dinner here, I imagine the shepherd's ghost coming back to have a look round. I suppose if he peeped in and saw me sitting here alone, in a dinner jacket, drinking champagne and being waited on by Watkins, he would think it a disgusting spectacle.' He paused for a split second, before adding, 'As indeed it is.' "

Indeed it may have been, but the story pinpoints the drama behind the surface of *What a Life!*: the conflict between our fascination with the appurtenances of physical comfort, that always seem to hold out the promise of a better life, and our knowledge that neither they nor anything else is going to alter the facts of existence on earth. One of this century's greatest poets, Osip Mandel-

stam, wrote in a letter from Switzerland in 1906: "I have
strange taste: I love the patches of reflected light on Lake
Leman, respectful lackeys, the silent flight of the elevator,
the marble vestibule of the hotel and the Englishwomen
who play Mozart with two or three official listeners in
the half-darkened salon. I love bourgeois, European comfort and am devoted to it not only physically but emo-
tionally." Yet his "devotion" never allowed him to aban-
don the poetry which eventually led him to death in a
Siberian prison camp after years of hardship. This tragic
ambivalence—the contradictory allegiances to physical
and spiritual well-being—exists in all of us and is the
core of the situation which Lucas and Morrow elaborated
within the confines of their exiguous comic masterpiece.
What a life, indeed.

JOHN ASHBERY

Cover from the original edition.

WHAT A LIFE !

AN AUTOBIOGRAPHY

BY

E. V. L. AND G. M.

ILLUSTRATED BY WHITELEY'S

UNION IS STRENGTH

Title page from the original edition.

PREFACE

A S adventures are to the adventurous, so is romance to the romantic. One man searching the pages of Whiteley's General Catalogue will find only facts and prices; another will find what we think we have found—a deeply-moving human drama.

E. V. L.

G. M.

CONTENTS

CHAPTER I

CHILDHOOD

I was born very near the end of the year.

The grange where I was born was situated in a secluded corner of the Chiltern Hills. Rumour had it that Queen Elizabeth had slept there.

My father was the soul of hospitality,

and kept cigars to suit all tastes.

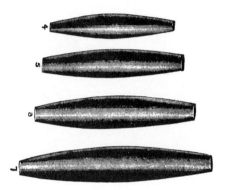

Never a very strong man,

he was perforce a
great traveller, and
my sweet mother
loved to follow his
wanderings on the
quaint old globe in
the library.

Their's was an ideal union. They were sweethearts since the time my mother wore short frocks.

Our house had superb grounds, and the garden was a scene of savage grandeur.

Two swans — one English and one Australian—were always on the lake.

Our head keeper—good fellow!—saw to
it that the birds were plentiful.

My father was not only a dead shot,

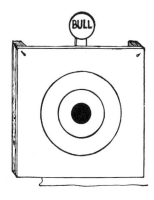

but, as a huntsman, frequently returned
home after a long day with the harriers,

tired but triumphant, with the brush.

My earliest recollection is of lying in the cradle and wondering if lying was my destiny.

Of all my nurses, Gregson was my favourite.

She was the daughter of a poor broken-down clarionet player, but was really a lady in spite of her garb of servitude.

Her parents lived in a Tudor manor that was reported to be haunted.

According to the legend whispered by the retainers and villagers, no sooner did the clock strike twelve

CHILDHOOD

Everyone was kind to me. Our Dutch gardener adored me,  and I prime fav with ou housekeep

But my happiest hours were spent with the little daughter of our neighbour Sir Easton West. She was a pretty child, and, boy-like, I did my best to attract her attention.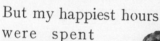

than a headless apparition was seen to move slowly across the moonlit hall.

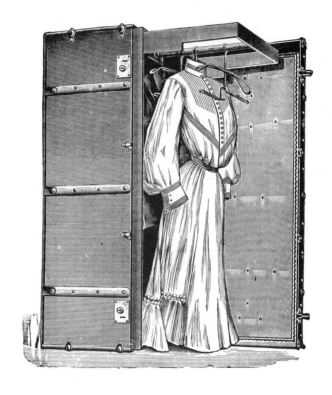

Poor Belinda, her fits were frequent.

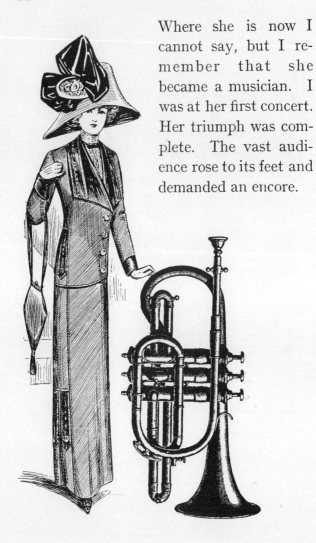

Where she is now I
cannot say, but I re-
member that she
became a musician. I
was at her first concert.
Her triumph was com-
plete. The vast audi-
ence rose to its feet and
demanded an encore.

I pass over other ordinary occurrences incidental to childhood, such as being kidnapped by gipsies,

and my first visit to the dentist,

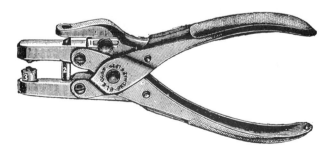

and come to my life at the preparatory school, to which I went to discover whether

WHAT A LIFE!

I was to serve my country in the Navy or
the Army.

Chapter II

SCHOOL DAYS

SCHOOL DAYS! Was there ever a happier time? I was sent to Dr. Bodey's in West Kensington.

The name was on the door—"Dryburgh." You could not mistake it.

Although a martyr to kidney trouble for

years, Dr. Bodey was a powerful man and
an adept at all outdoor sports.

He had married a Swiss, a lady as active as himself,

and together they held the championship at Spiro-pole.

A lenient and generous teacher, the Doctor took us often to the Crystal Palace

or to the Zoo.

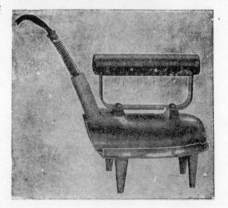

Our favourite game was leapfrog.

I was at this time a handsome boy of fourteen.

Among my school fellows were some delightful lads,

chiefly the sons of the nobility and clergy.

My closest friend was
Eustace Bleek-Wether
with whom I often
spent the vacations;

and my *bête noire* was
the Hon. Harold
Crumpton, who made
my life at school a
perfect hell for the first
three months.

His father was a learned and interesting man, with, alas, one sad and only too common failing.

They lived in a beautiful home nestling in the Surrey hills.

We both adored
the matron.

In spite of this rivalry we were friends, and remained so after leaving Dr. Bodey's and passing through the 'Varsity.

Eustace was brilliant in every way. A
wonderful fisherman ;

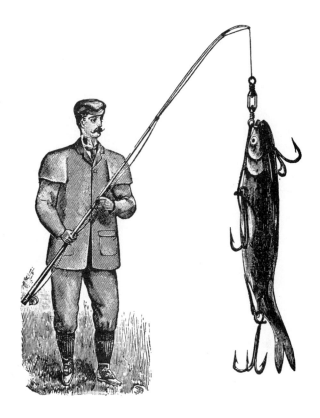

and a crack shot, rarely bringing down his birds singly.

Once, however, (I remember) he missed his
quarry.   Time after time he fired, but the
bird was still there.

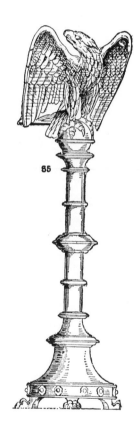

Poor Eustace! a fatal fascination for the
Pole gripped him,

and he now lies in a silent grave beneath
the Arctic star.

To return to my own story, I left school when I was eighteen and went to Oxford College,

and
at the
age   of
t w e n t y -
two I became
a man about
town with a latch-key of my own.

Chapter III

LONDON IN THE OLD DAYS

KNOCKING about town as I then did, I naturally got to know many people, especially as I was still unmarried.

For example, Lady Mayfair, the present Queen of Society, I remember as a little toddling child who climbed on my knees.

I knew Monty Wotherspoon, the amateur pyramid champion, intimately.

Monty was one of the old dare-devil crowd. I remember the sensation he caused when, for a wager, he drove a hansom from the Guards' Club to Hurlingham without reins.

Poor fellow, his end was very tragic. He was poisoned by his wife. She had rinsed the glass and removed, as she thought, all traces of the poison ; but the Law was too much for her.

A, SERVICE PIPE FROM MAIN
B, INLET TO FILTER
C, OUTLET OF FILTERED. WATER
D, FLUSH TAP
E, ORDINARY WATER TAP.

The autopsy revealed unmistakable signs of the deadly drug.

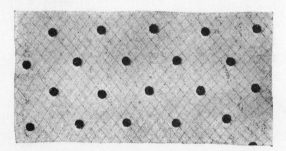

Then there was the Earl of Crewett, who was never seen out of riding breeches: a veritable centaur.

It was Lord Crewett who won the Derby with "Salad Days."

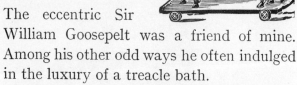

The eccentric Sir William Goosepelt was a friend of mine. Among his other odd ways he often indulged in the luxury of a treacle bath.

Sir William's ears were so large that he required a chin-strap to keep his hat on. From this circum-
stance he earned an unenviable reputation for im-politeness towards ladies.

His wife, dear Lady Goosepelt, was a chronic invalid, and lived at Bournemouth in a charming *villegiatura*.

Sir William's beautiful mansion was burnt to the ground. It was, I remember, on Sunday, the 23rd.

The alarm was given, but no horses could be procured, so the brigade was at a standstill.

Another man about town at that time was Sir Henry Punt. He and his wife (a beautiful woman) were probably the most inveterate gamblers living.

Lady Punt was one of the few women of fashion who had received the King's Bounty, and I often watched her charming brood bathing in the marble basin in their grounds, which adjoined mine.

Sir Henry (who died only last year) had a weakness for growing mushrooms for harvest festivals.

The Duke of Pudsey, in spite of his great wealth, was of a penurious nature. He was also something of a kleptomaniac, and after his death an extraordinary collection of umbrellas which he had removed from the club stand was discovered.

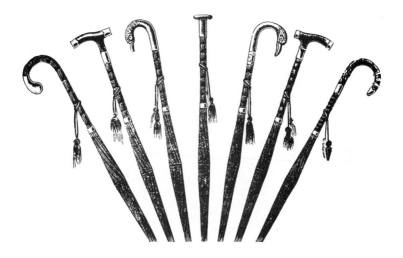

On one occasion he was actually found concealing the watch of one of his guests,

None the less (such is human tolerance of
the great), when the Duke came to die a
magnificent memorial was erected to him.

His son's wife, Lady Clipstone, was one of the most determined autograph hunters I ever met.

The Duke's only daughter, who became Lady Grapholine Meadows, was never seen without her coronet, which was a masterpiece of the jeweller's art.

His other son, Lord Bertie, married the fashionable sister of Lord George Sangazure.

It was about this time that I made the acquaintance of William Browne, of London,

whose peculiarity it was to be always
out. It is con-
jectured that
during a period
of many years
he was never at
home.

Sir William Broadfoot, the well-known
R.A., was a frequent visitor. He would
often go out sketching, but was so absent-
minded that he forgot his paints.

Then there was Lord Highlow, who con-
structed a dirigible of his own invention, in
which he made fre-
quent ascents from
Brooklands, accom-
panied by his two
beautiful daughters.

Stanley
Herne, the
motor cycle
champion,
was also a
friend of mine.
Alas ! he rides no more, not since that
terrible collision with a motor bus.   There

lay Stanley, a ruin of what he was, while
the heavy vehicle, crowded with happy
passengers, all unconscious of what had
happened, rolled on.

I knew slightly Sir Algernon
Slack, the millionaire, whose
peculiarity it was never to
carry an umbrella.

One of this strange man's peculiarities
was that he could not endure the presence
of a cat.

His end, it is thought, was quickened by varicose veins in the right hand.

He died in 1901, and was buried next his wife.

Chapter IV

THE STOLEN DIAMONDS

ONE of the most interesting occurrences of my crowded life was my participation in the famous Closure Castle jewel robbery.

I was staying with Lord Bunderbourne. His old Jacobean mansion embowered in trees was an ideal spot for a daring burglary.

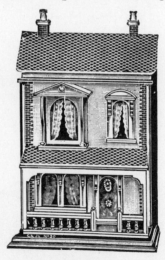

It was, I remember, mid-
winter. The fountain was
frozen.

We had just finished dinner

when the local constable
burst in to say that a convict
had escaped from the neigh-
bouring prison.

It was too true.   The safe was empty.

Our cigars were forgotten in the excitement
of the moment.

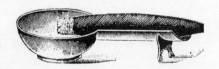

A detective was telephoned for, and came at once.

He first made a plan of the house,

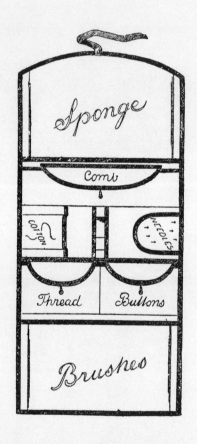

and hurried next to the kitchen garden, where he stood aghast at his discovery.

Then on to the out-houses, where it was noticed that one of the doors was partly open.

Ponto, the watch dog, seemed dazed. He had been drugged, the detective said.

He also pointed out that the horse's neck was strangely swollen.

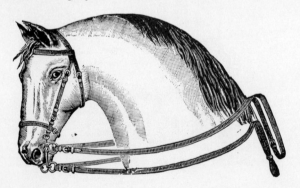

The detective next interrogated the whole house party, although some were in *déshabille*.

Suspicion fell first on the chief footman, whose embarrass- ment was greatly in his disfavour.

Passing to the man's room the detective saw at a glance that the bed had not been slept on.

Meanwhile, being alone in the drawing room, I had an instinctive feeling that someone was hiding behind the screen,

and I was certain
that I heard the
sound of the
sharpening of a
knife.

Having no other weapon handy, I produced
my toothpick.

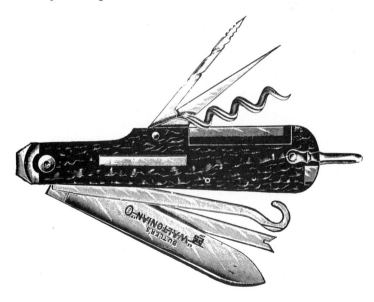

But at this moment the detective returned, in a disguise calculated to baffle the keenest observer.

The contents of the mysterious bag having been analysed,

he showed us that the ring was movable,

and drew our attention to the fact that there were signs of a struggle.

He then showed us the print of a blood-stained hand on the wall,

and producing his pocket book, convinced
us that in spite of certain superficial
differences, they were one and the same
man.

We were immensely impressed, and in a
few moments the burglar was fairly trapped.

The detective then resumed his natural appearance,

and was presented by Lord Bunderbourne with a heavy cheque.

While waiting for the prison van

he told us some
good stories of
his career. It was
he, it seems, who
was the real hero
of the Charlotte
Street anarchist
plot, which he dis-
covered by over-
hearing a conversa-
tion between two
of the miscreants in
a Soho restaurant.

He gave us also some curious information about the in-genious methods of famous c r i m i n a l s. There was, for example, the notorious one-eyed Jimmy Snaffles, who used a house-breaking implement of his own construction, which he would try on the trees outside before breaking into the house.

And there were that very respectable couple, Tom Bilks and his wife, who entered houses with scaling ladders at night, and kept a blameless registry office in Balham through the day.

CHAPTER V

THE TENDER PASSION

It is idle to deny that I was a hand- some man.

Some-
thing also
of a dandy,
my appeal
to women must have been terrific.

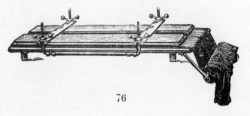

76

They were also attracted by my Norman descent, for it was common knowledge that one of my ancestors, Sir Ikimo de Medici, had come over with the Conqueror.

Always susceptible, I quickly fell in love. My first *innamorata* was the daughter of a lion tamer, and herself, although a Suffragette, in that romantic profession.

Her father disapproved of the intimacy, and
we had to correspond clandestinely.   She
would write and seal her letter, and then
place it inside a football, and leave it for me
in the place agreed upon.

My second love was the lady golf
champion of Golder's Green.

Dear Honoria — she inherited from her
uncle, Sir Felix Chalk-
stones, one of the neatest
ankles in the Home
Counties.

Unfortunately she was a deaf mute, and
when we met our sweet
nothings had to be con-
veyed by the clumsy
method of sign language.

My third was Lily,
who never wrote, but
communicated with me
on the telephone.

—Dear, brave Lily, who in the dark days struggled so hard to support her mother and poor ailing Susan.

But at last I met my fate—Lady Brenda
Birdseye. I had motored over to her
father's seat—Cavendish Court. I wandered
through the house; it was empty. Lunch
was not yet cleared away.

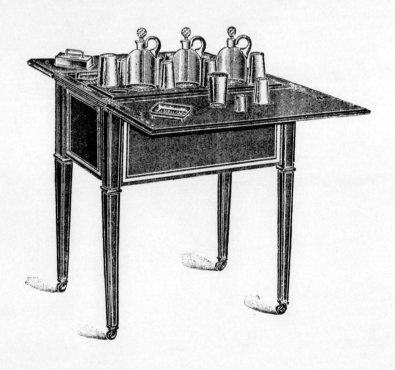

The tennis court was deserted ;

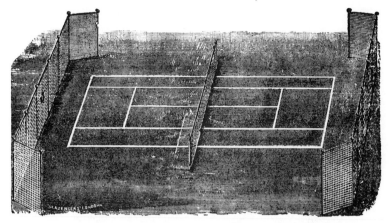

but in a hammock in the shrubbery I chanced upon her—asleep. It seemed a pity to disturb her dreams. I gazed, and was fascinated.

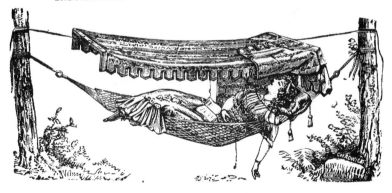

Fond fool—I thought that Lady Brenda smiled upon me. She seemed to like me to pay for her lunch. We were often to be seen together at Ranelagh.

But I was living in a fool's paradise—she loved another. The news came to me as I was eating my breakfast.

Could it be true? But to whom was she engaged? To Lord Kempton, that cur.

What was I to do ?   To hail and leap into a taxi was the work of a moment.

The maid said she was not at home. I said I *must* see her. She saw me. I heard afterwards how she had braced herself for the effort.

I vowed to be revenged on my rival, even if I had to follow him to the bottom of the sea.

She gave me no hope and I left her in despair. For days I lived on nothing but a few sandwiches.

Then I grew more philosophic and tried other means to forget her,

but in vain. It was no good, I took to my bed; and for some months my life was despaired of.

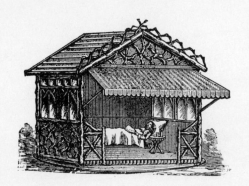

On recovering sufficiently, I determined to seek peace of mind in travel.

Chapter VI

TRAVEL AND ADVENTURE

IN the mad effort to forget Lady Brenda
I globe-trotted furiously.

One day found me among the quaint
walled towns of Normandy.

The next I was in Germany.

Feeling that excitement was necessary to me, I joined the motor race to Monte Carlo,

and was to be seen every night in the Casino ;

where I lost heavily.

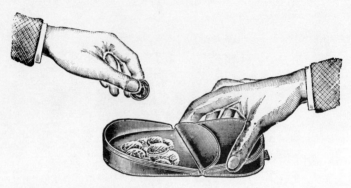

I passed on to Venice,

and from there to Naples.

But in vain—I could not forget Lady Brenda, and sleep was out of the question.

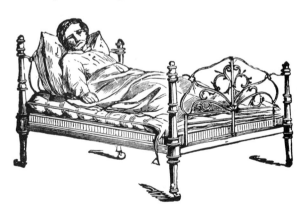

I also suffered from loss of **memory**, and frequently forgot my shirt and waist-coat.

In my despair I took for a brief, mad period to drink, but was careful that no one should suspect the proximity of the bottle.

From Naples I passed on to India, that land

of mystery
and Eastern
splendour.

It was my first
experience of the
tropics.   The heat
was intense.

At night I lay with my tent open;

by day the jungle throbbed beneath the
intolerable sun.

But by taking precautions I retained my
health.

I had also my faithful and admirable syce,
who, like everyone with whom I have
ever come in contact (except, alas! Lady
Brenda), adored
me.

Then came the
Paticaka Guerilla
War. I enlisted
against the insurgent
Gherkins.

I slept soundly the
night before the
battle.

Although shot many times I fought on, but I became unconscious from loss of blood, not, however, until the day was won. That night eleven bullets, which I still preserve, were extracted from my body.

The Maharajah showed his appreciation of my services,

and, furthermore, put me to the blush by offering me his favourite wife.

It was on leaving Paticaka that I had the narrowest escape from death that I have yet experienced.   I took my seat in the Calcutta train

and settled myself to repose, when, with a fearful crash, the carriage was overturned. We had disregarded the signal.

The scene was appalling; human remains strewed the ground.

Fortunately I escaped unhurt, although somewhat badly shaken.

Before returning to England I visited Japan,

where I made many friends among the quaint little people. I saw a sight I shall never forget—the sun rising over Fusiyama.

Later in the day I saw it set—an equally
memorable spectacle.

AFTER USE

From Japan I sailed to Africa, and among
the many photographs I took is a view of a
kraal on the banks of the Oomba river,
Nygskmbasi, B.C.A.

CHAPTER VII

HOME LIFE

I T was on the liner coming back,

just off (I remember) the Eddystone light-
house,

that I met my dear wife.

She was the daughter of a retired Govern-
ment official, now

enjoying a leisurely and happy old age.

We had long been catching each other's eyes. The time was ripe. When I at last proposed, she gave me both hands impulsively.

Ours was a romantic engagement,

but we decided to cut it very short, and were
married directly the
village church could
be made ready.

We had some very novel wedding
presents.

My best man was Lord Wagglecleek.

Almost my oldest friend, I
had first met him in the bath.

It was a pretty service, and the villagers,
whose hearts are wholly ours,

gave us a cordial send-off.

We were idyllically happy at Frisby Towers, in spite of its outward air of gloom.

We both had rural tastes.   My wife was very fond of whipping the stream, and I was, of course, an ardent golfer.

One day we took the motor;

on the next I ordered out the roan.

When it rained we knew what to do.

We were so simple that we often did not dress for dinner.

In the evening after a small but *recherché*
meal, for the *cuisine* at Frisby Towers left
nothing to be desired,

we had music.   Melba's divine notes floated
into the liquid air,

or I would perform
a solo on my favour-
ite   instrument,
which I flatter my-
self I play with a
certain amount of
delicacy and feeling ;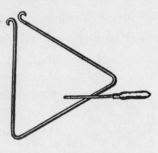

my wife occasionally ac-
companying me on the
harp.

We entertained freely.
Like my father I am a most
hospitable man.

No sooner is a guest
inside my doors, than I
pass the refreshments.

In other
ways also I
kept them
amused
and happy.

By day we often made up parties of six for
the fishing.

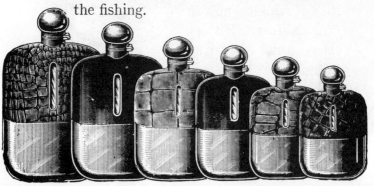

I had my hobbies too.   In 1904 I suc-
ceeded, after
many failures,
in obtaining a
cross between
a tortoise and
a porcupine,
and the train-
ing of the hybrid gives me infinite
pleasure.

I was also the foremost conchologist of
the country, and the
arranging of my col-
lection of 14,000 varie-
ties of winkles, now in
the Natural History
Museum, occupied
many otherwise
tedious evenings.

Life also had its
exciting incidents.
Now and then I
would add to my
unique collection
of Sèvres ;

or a new hat would
come from London
for my wife.

Sometimes a guest revoked;

while an occasional *fracas* with the plumber
also enlivened the routine, as when on one
memorable occasion I drew his attention to
the inadequacy of the bath.

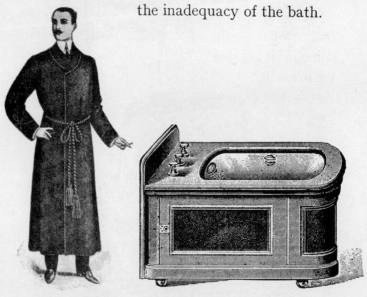

Now and then my wife and I may even have had a tiff, during which we were not on speaking terms ; but it soon blew over.

On Sunday we naturally went to church, to which, in my capacity of Squire, I pre-sented a new organ,

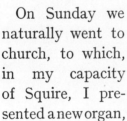

and where I frequently had the pleasure
of hearing the choir render my favourite
hymns.

Chapter VIII

APOTHEOSIS.

SUCH was my life for a considerable
period—, rendered really notable only
by the arrival of a son and heir—

until 1911, my *annus mirabilis*. But then
everything was changed, for the Prime
Minister graciously invited me to become

one of his new peers, which I was pleased to agree to ; and I therefore take my leave of my patient and too indulgent readers as Baron Dropmore, of Corfe.

A CATALOGUE OF SELECTED DOVER BOOKS
IN ALL FIELDS OF INTEREST

A CATALOGUE OF SELECTED DOVER BOOKS
IN ALL FIELDS OF INTEREST

AMERICA'S OLD MASTERS, James T. Flexner. Four men emerged unexpectedly from provincial 18th century America to leadership in European art: Benjamin West, J. S. Copley, C. R. Peale, Gilbert Stuart. Brilliant coverage of lives and contributions. Revised, 1967 edition. 69 plates. 365pp. of text.
21806-6 Paperbound $3.00

FIRST FLOWERS OF OUR WILDERNESS: AMERICAN PAINTING, THE COLONIAL PERIOD, James T. Flexner. Painters, and regional painting traditions from earliest Colonial times up to the emergence of Copley, West and Peale Sr., Foster, Gustavus Hesselius, Feke, John Smibert and many anonymous painters in the primitive manner. Engaging presentation, with 162 illustrations. xxii + 368pp.
22180-6 Paperbound $3.50

THE LIGHT OF DISTANT SKIES: AMERICAN PAINTING, 1760-1835, James T. Flexner. The great generation of early American painters goes to Europe to learn and to teach: West, Copley, Gilbert Stuart and others. Allston, Trumbull, Morse; also contemporary American painters—primitives, derivatives, academics—who remained in America. 102 illustrations. xiii + 306pp.
22179-2 Paperbound $3.50

A HISTORY OF THE RISE AND PROGRESS OF THE ARTS OF DESIGN IN THE UNITED STATES, William Dunlap. Much the richest mine of information on early American painters, sculptors, architects, engravers, miniaturists, etc. The only source of information for scores of artists, the major primary source for many others. Unabridged reprint of rare original 1834 edition, with new introduction by James T. Flexner, and 394 new illustrations. Edited by Rita Weiss. 6⅝ x 9⅝.
21695-0, 21696-9, 21697-7 Three volumes, Paperbound $15.00

EPOCHS OF CHINESE AND JAPANESE ART, Ernest F. Fenollosa. From primitive Chinese art to the 20th century, thorough history, explanation of every important art period and form, including Japanese woodcuts; main stress on China and Japan, but Tibet, Korea also included. Still unexcelled for its detailed, rich coverage of cultural background, aesthetic elements, diffusion studies, particularly of the historical period. 2nd, 1913 edition. 242 illustrations. lii + 439pp. of text.
20364-6, 20365-4 Two volumes, Paperbound $6.00

THE GENTLE ART OF MAKING ENEMIES, James A. M. Whistler. Greatest wit of his day deflates Oscar Wilde, Ruskin, Swinburne; strikes back at inane critics, exhibitions, art journalism; aesthetics of impressionist revolution in most striking form. Highly readable classic by great painter. Reproduction of edition designed by Whistler. Introduction by Alfred Werner. xxxvi + 334pp.
21875-9 Paperbound $3.00

DESIGN BY ACCIDENT; A BOOK OF "ACCIDENTAL EFFECTS" FOR ARTISTS AND DESIGNERS, James F. O'Brien. Create your own unique, striking, imaginative effects by "controlled accident" interaction of materials: paints and lacquers, oil and water based paints, splatter, crackling materials, shatter, similar items. Everything you do will be different; first book on this limitless art, so useful to both fine artist and commercial artist. Full instructions. 192 plates showing "accidents," 8 in color. viii + 215pp. 8⅜ x 11¼. 21942-9 Paperbound $3.75

THE BOOK OF SIGNS, Rudolf Koch. Famed German type designer draws 493 beautiful symbols: religious, mystical, alchemical, imperial, property marks, runes, etc. Remarkable fusion of traditional and modern. Good for suggestions of timelessness, smartness, modernity. Text. vi + 104pp. 6⅛ x 9¼.
20162-7 Paperbound $1.50

HISTORY OF INDIAN AND INDONESIAN ART, Ananda K. Coomaraswamy. An unabridged republication of one of the finest books by a great scholar in Eastern art. Rich in descriptive material, history, social backgrounds; Sunga reliefs, Rajput paintings, Gupta temples, Burmese frescoes, textiles, jewelry, sculpture, etc. 400 photos. viii + 423pp. 6⅜ x 9¾. 21436-2 Paperbound $5.00

PRIMITIVE ART, Franz Boas. America's foremost anthropologist surveys textiles, ceramics, woodcarving, basketry, metalwork, etc.; patterns, technology, creation of symbols, style origins. All areas of world, but very full on Northwest Coast Indians. More than 350 illustrations of baskets, boxes, totem poles, weapons, etc. 378 pp.
20025-6 Paperbound $3.00

THE GENTLEMAN AND CABINET MAKER'S DIRECTOR, Thomas Chippendale. Full reprint (third edition, 1762) of most influential furniture book of all time, by master cabinetmaker. 200 plates, illustrating chairs, sofas, mirrors, tables, cabinets, plus 24 photographs of surviving pieces. Biographical introduction by N. Bienenstock. vi + 249pp. 9⅞ x 12¾. 21601-2 Paperbound $5.00

AMERICAN ANTIQUE FURNITURE, Edgar G. Miller, Jr. The basic coverage of all American furniture before 1840. Individual chapters cover type of furniture—clocks, tables, sideboards, etc.—chronologically, with inexhaustible wealth of data. More than 2100 photographs, all identified, commented on. Essential to all early American collectors. Introduction by H. E. Keyes. vi + 1106pp. 7⅞ x 10¾.
21599-7, 21600-4 Two volumes, Paperbound $11.00

PENNSYLVANIA DUTCH AMERICAN FOLK ART, Henry J. Kauffman. 279 photos, 28 drawings of tulipware, Fraktur script, painted tinware, toys, flowered furniture, quilts, samplers, hex signs, house interiors, etc. Full descriptive text. Excellent for tourist, rewarding for designer, collector. Map. 146pp. 7⅞ x 10¾.
21205-X Paperbound $3.00

EARLY NEW ENGLAND GRAVESTONE RUBBINGS, Edmund V. Gillon, Jr. 43 photographs, 226 carefully reproduced rubbings show heavily symbolic, sometimes macabre early gravestones, up to early 19th century. Remarkable early American primitive art, occasionally strikingly beautiful; always powerful. Text. xxvi + 207pp. 8⅜ x 11¼. 21380-3 Paperbound $4.00

LAST AND FIRST MEN AND STAR MAKER, TWO SCIENCE FICTION NOVELS, Olaf Stapledon. Greatest future histories in science fiction. In the first, human intelligence is the "hero," through strange paths of evolution, interplanetary invasions, incredible technologies, near extinctions and reemergences. Star Maker describes the quest of a band of star rovers for intelligence itself, through time and space: weird inhuman civilizations, crustacean minds, symbiotic worlds, etc. Complete, unabridged. v + 438pp. (USO) 21962-3 Paperbound $3.00

THREE PROPHETIC NOVELS, H. G. WELLS. Stages of a consistently planned future for mankind. *When the Sleeper Wakes,* and *A Story of the Days to Come,* anticipate *Brave New World* and *1984,* in the 21st Century; *The Time Machine,* only complete version in print, shows farther future and the end of mankind. All show Wells's greatest gifts as storyteller and novelist. Edited by E. F. Bleiler. x + 335pp. (USO) 20605-X Paperbound $3.00

THE DEVIL'S DICTIONARY, Ambrose Bierce. America's own Oscar Wilde—Ambrose Bierce—offers his barbed iconoclastic wisdom in over 1,000 definitions hailed by H. L. Mencken as "some of the most gorgeous witticisms in the English language." 145pp. 20487-1 Paperbound $1.50

MAX AND MORITZ, Wilhelm Busch. Great children's classic, father of comic strip, of two bad boys, Max and Moritz. Also Ker and Plunk (Plisch und Plumm), Cat and Mouse, Deceitful Henry, Ice-Peter, The Boy and the Pipe, and five other pieces. Original German, with English translation. Edited by H. Arthur Klein; translations by various hands and H. Arthur Klein. vi + 216pp. 20181-3 Paperbound $2.00

PIGS IS PIGS AND OTHER FAVORITES, Ellis Parker Butler. The title story is one of the best humor short stories, as Mike Flannery obfuscates biology and English. Also included, That Pup of Murchison's, The Great American Pie Company, and Perkins of Portland. 14 illustrations. v + 109pp. 21532-6 Paperbound $1.50

THE PETERKIN PAPERS, Lucretia P. Hale. It takes genius to be as stupidly mad as the Peterkins, as they decide to become wise, celebrate the "Fourth," keep a cow, and otherwise strain the resources of the Lady from Philadelphia. Basic book of American humor. 153 illustrations. 219pp. 20794-3 Paperbound $2.00

PERRAULT'S FAIRY TALES, translated by A. E. Johnson and S. R. Littlewood, with 34 full-page illustrations by Gustave Doré. All the original Perrault stories—Cinderella, Sleeping Beauty, Bluebeard, Little Red Riding Hood, Puss in Boots, Tom Thumb, etc.—with their witty verse morals and the magnificent illustrations of Doré. One of the five or six great books of European fairy tales. viii + 117pp. 8⅛ x 11. 22311-6 Paperbound $2.00

OLD HUNGARIAN FAIRY TALES, Baroness Orczy. Favorites translated and adapted by author of the *Scarlet Pimpernel.* Eight fairy tales include "The Suitors of Princess Fire-Fly," "The Twin Hunchbacks," "Mr. Cuttlefish's Love Story," and "The Enchanted Cat." This little volume of magic and adventure will captivate children as it has for generations. 90 drawings by Montagu Barstow. 96pp. (USO) 22293-4 Paperbound $1.95

EAST O' THE SUN AND WEST O' THE MOON, George W. Dasent. Considered the best of all translations of these Norwegian folk tales, this collection has been enjoyed by generations of children (and folklorists too). Includes True and Untrue, Why the Sea is Salt, East O' the Sun and West O' the Moon, Why the Bear is Stumpy-Tailed, Boots and the Troll, The Cock and the Hen, Rich Peter the Pedlar, and 52 more. The only edition with all 59 tales. 77 illustrations by Erik Werenskiold and Theodor Kittelsen. xv + 418pp. 22521-6 Paperbound $3.50

GOOPS AND HOW TO BE THEM, Gelett Burgess. Classic of tongue-in-cheek humor, masquerading as etiquette book. 87 verses, twice as many cartoons, show mischievous Goops as they demonstrate to children virtues of table manners, neatness, courtesy, etc. Favorite for generations. viii + 88pp. 6½ x 9¼. 22233-0 Paperbound $1.50

ALICE'S ADVENTURES UNDER GROUND, Lewis Carroll. The first version, quite different from the final Alice in Wonderland, printed out by Carroll himself with his own illustrations. Complete facsimile of the "million dollar" manuscript Carroll gave to Alice Liddell in 1864. Introduction by Martin Gardner. viii + 96pp. Title and dedication pages in color. 21482-6 Paperbound $1.25

THE BROWNIES, THEIR BOOK, Palmer Cox. Small as mice, cunning as foxes, exuberant and full of mischief, the Brownies go to the zoo, toy shop, seashore, circus, etc., in 24 verse adventures and 266 illustrations. Long a favorite, since their first appearance in St. Nicholas Magazine. xi + 144pp. 6⅝ x 9¼. 21265-3 Paperbound $1.75

SONGS OF CHILDHOOD, Walter De La Mare. Published (under the pseudonym Walter Ramal) when De La Mare was only 29, this charming collection has long been a favorite children's book. A facsimile of the first edition in paper, the 47 poems capture the simplicity of the nursery rhyme and the ballad, including such lyrics as I Met Eve, Tartary, The Silver Penny. vii + 106pp. (USO) 21972-0 Paperbound $1.25

THE COMPLETE NONSENSE OF EDWARD LEAR, Edward Lear. The finest 19th-century humorist-cartoonist in full: all nonsense limericks, zany alphabets, Owl and Pussycat, songs, nonsense botany, and more than 500 illustrations by Lear himself. Edited by Holbrook Jackson. xxix + 287pp. (USO) 20167-8 Paperbound $2.00

BILLY WHISKERS: THE AUTOBIOGRAPHY OF A GOAT, Frances Trego Montgomery. A favorite of children since the early 20th century, here are the escapades of that rambunctious, irresistible and mischievous goat—Billy Whiskers. Much in the spirit of Peck's Bad Boy, this is a book that children never tire of reading or hearing. All the original familiar illustrations by W. H. Fry are included: 6 color plates, 18 black and white drawings. 159pp. 22345-0 Paperbound $2.00

MOTHER GOOSE MELODIES. Faithful republication of the fabulously rare Munroe and Francis "copyright 1833" Boston edition—the most important Mother Goose collection, usually referred to as the "original." Familiar rhymes plus many rare ones, with wonderful old woodcut illustrations. Edited by E. F. Bleiler. 128pp. 4½ x 6⅜. 22577-1 Paperbound $1.00

TWO LITTLE SAVAGES; BEING THE ADVENTURES OF TWO BOYS WHO LIVED AS INDIANS AND WHAT THEY LEARNED, Ernest Thompson Seton. Great classic of nature and boyhood provides a vast range of woodlore in most palatable form, a genuinely entertaining story. Two farm boys build a teepee in woods and live in it for a month, working out Indian solutions to living problems, star lore, birds and animals, plants, etc. 293 illustrations. vii + 286pp.

20985-7 Paperbound $2.50

PETER PIPER'S PRACTICAL PRINCIPLES OF PLAIN & PERFECT PRONUNCIATION. Alliterative jingles and tongue-twisters of surprising charm, that made their first appearance in America about 1830. Republished in full with the spirited woodcut illustrations from this earliest American edition. 32pp. $4\frac{1}{2}$ x $6\frac{3}{8}$.

22560-7 Paperbound $1.00

SCIENCE EXPERIMENTS AND AMUSEMENTS FOR CHILDREN, Charles Vivian. 73 easy experiments, requiring only materials found at home or easily available, such as candles, coins, steel wool, etc.; illustrate basic phenomena like vacuum, simple chemical reaction, etc. All safe. Modern, well-planned. Formerly *Science Games for Children*. 102 photos, numerous drawings. 96pp. $6\frac{1}{8}$ x $9\frac{1}{4}$.

21856-2 Paperbound $1.25

AN INTRODUCTION TO CHESS MOVES AND TACTICS SIMPLY EXPLAINED, Leonard Barden. Informal intermediate introduction, quite strong in explaining reasons for moves. Covers basic material, tactics, important openings, traps, positional play in middle game, end game. Attempts to isolate patterns and recurrent configurations. Formerly *Chess*. 58 figures. 102pp.   (USO) 21210-6 Paperbound $1.25

LASKER'S MANUAL OF CHESS, Dr. Emanuel Lasker. Lasker was not only one of the five great World Champions, he was also one of the ablest expositors, theorists, and analysts. In many ways, his Manual, permeated with his philosophy of battle, filled with keen insights, is one of the greatest works ever written on chess. Filled with analyzed games by the great players. A single-volume library that will profit almost any chess player, beginner or master. 308 diagrams. xli x 349pp.

20640-8 Paperbound $2.75

THE MASTER BOOK OF MATHEMATICAL RECREATIONS, Fred Schuh. In opinion of many the finest work ever prepared on mathematical puzzles, stunts, recreations; exhaustively thorough explanations of mathematics involved, analysis of effects, citation of puzzles and games. Mathematics involved is elementary. Translated by F. Göbel. 194 figures. xxiv + 430pp.   22134-2 Paperbound $4.00

MATHEMATICS, MAGIC AND MYSTERY, Martin Gardner. Puzzle editor for Scientific American explains mathematics behind various mystifying tricks: card tricks, stage "mind reading," coin and match tricks, counting out games, geometric dissections, etc. Probability sets, theory of numbers clearly explained. Also provides more than 400 tricks, guaranteed to work, that you can do. 135 illustrations. xii + 176pp.

20335-2 Paperbound $2.00

AMERICAN FOOD AND GAME FISHES, David S. Jordan and Barton W. Evermann. Definitive source of information, detailed and accurate enough to enable the sportsman and nature lover to identify conclusively some 1,000 species and sub-species of North American fish, sought for food or sport. Coverage of range, physiology, habits, life history, food value. Best methods of capture, interest to the angler, advice on bait, fly-fishing, etc. 338 drawings and photographs. 1 + 574pp. 6⅝ x 9⅜.
22196-2 Paperbound $5.00

THE FROG BOOK, Mary C. Dickerson. Complete with extensive finding keys, over 300 photographs, and an introduction to the general biology of frogs and toads, this is the classic non-technical study of Northeastern and Central species. 58 species; 290 photographs and 16 color plates. xvii + 253pp.
21973-9 Paperbound $4.00

THE MOTH BOOK: A GUIDE TO THE MOTHS OF NORTH AMERICA, William J. Holland. Classical study, eagerly sought after and used for the past 60 years. Clear identification manual to more than 2,000 different moths, largest manual in existence. General information about moths, capturing, mounting, classifying, etc., followed by species by species descriptions. 263 illustrations plus 48 color plates show almost every species, full size. 1968 edition, preface, nomenclature changes by A. E. Brower. xxiv + 479pp. of text. 6½ x 9¼.
21948-8 Paperbound $6.00

THE SEA-BEACH AT EBB-TIDE, Augusta Foote Arnold. Interested amateur can identify hundreds of marine plants and animals on coasts of North America; marine algae; seaweeds; squids; hermit crabs; horse shoe crabs; shrimps; corals; sea anemones; etc. Species descriptions cover: structure; food; reproductive cycle; size; shape; color; habitat; etc. Over 600 drawings. 85 plates. xii + 490pp.
21949-6 Paperbound $4.00

COMMON BIRD SONGS, Donald J. Borror. 33⅓ 12-inch record presents songs of 60 important birds of the eastern United States. A thorough, serious record which provides several examples for each bird, showing different types of song, individual variations, etc. Inestimable identification aid for birdwatcher. 32-page booklet gives text about birds and songs, with illustration for each bird.
21829-5 Record, book, album. Monaural. $3.50

FADS AND FALLACIES IN THE NAME OF SCIENCE, Martin Gardner. Fair, witty appraisal of cranks and quacks of science: Atlantis, Lemuria, hollow earth, flat earth, Velikovsky, orgone energy, Dianetics, flying saucers, Bridey Murphy, food fads, medical fads, perpetual motion, etc. Formerly "In the Name of Science." x + 363pp.
20394-8 Paperbound $3.00

HOAXES, Curtis D. MacDougall. Exhaustive, unbelievably rich account of great hoaxes: Locke's moon hoax, Shakespearean forgeries, sea serpents, Loch Ness monster, Cardiff giant, John Wilkes Booth's mummy, Disumbrationist school of art, dozens more; also journalism, psychology of hoaxing. 54 illustrations. xi + 338pp.
20465-0 Paperbound $3.50

VISUAL ILLUSIONS: THEIR CAUSES, CHARACTERISTICS, AND APPLICATIONS, Matthew Luckiesh. Thorough description and discussion of optical illusion, geometric and perspective, particularly; size and shape distortions, illusions of color, of motion; natural illusions; use of illusion in art and magic, industry, etc. Most useful today with op art, also for classical art. Scores of effects illustrated. Introduction by William H. ⸱ ⸳eson. 100 illustrations. xxi + 252pp.

21530-X Paperbound $2.00

A HANDBOOK OF ANATOMY FOR ART STUDENTS, Arthur Thomson. Thorough, virtually exhaustive coverage of skeletal structure, musculature, etc. Full text, supplemented by anatomical diagrams and drawings and by photographs of undraped figures. Unique in its comparison of male and female forms, pointing out differences of contour, texture, form. 211 figures, 40 drawings, 86 photographs. xx + 459pp. 5⅜ x 8⅜.

21163-0 Paperbound $3.50

150 MASTERPIECES OF DRAWING, Selected by Anthony Toney. Full page reproductions of drawings from the early 16th to the end of the 18th century, all beautifully reproduced: Rembrandt, Michelangelo, Dürer, Fragonard, Urs, Graf, Wouwerman, many others. First-rate browsing book, model book for artists. xviii + 150pp. 8⅜ x 11¼.

21032-4 Paperbound $2.50

THE LATER WORK OF AUBREY BEARDSLEY, Aubrey Beardsley. Exotic, erotic, ironic masterpieces in full maturity: Comedy Ballet, Venus and Tannhauser, Pierrot, Lysistrata, Rape of the Lock, Savoy material, Ali Baba, Volpone, etc. This material revolutionized the art world, and is still powerful, fresh, brilliant. With *The Early Work,* all Beardsley's finest work. 174 plates, 2 in color. xiv + 176pp. 8⅛ x 11.

21817-1 Paperbound $3.75

DRAWINGS OF REMBRANDT, Rembrandt van Rijn. Complete reproduction of fabulously rare edition by Lippmann and Hofstede de Groot, completely reedited, updated, improved by Prof. Seymour Slive, Fogg Museum. Portraits, Biblical sketches, landscapes, Oriental types, nudes, episodes from classical mythology—All Rembrandt's fertile genius. Also selection of drawings by his pupils and followers. "Stunning volumes," *Saturday Review.* 550 illustrations. lxxviii + 552pp. 9⅛ x 12¼.

21485-0, 21486-9 Two volumes, Paperbound $10.00

THE DISASTERS OF WAR, Francisco Goya. One of the masterpieces of Western civilization—83 etchings that record Goya's shattering, bitter reaction to the Napoleonic war that swept through Spain after the insurrection of 1808 and to war in general. Reprint of the first edition, with three additional plates from Boston's Museum of Fine Arts. All plates facsimile size. Introduction by Philip Hofer, Fogg Museum. v + 97pp. 9⅜ x 8¼.

21872-4 Paperbound $2.50

GRAPHIC WORKS OF ODILON REDON. Largest collection of Redon's graphic works ever assembled: 172 lithographs, 28 etchings and engravings, 9 drawings. These include some of his most famous works. All the plates from *Odilon Redon: oeuvre graphique complet,* plus additional plates. New introduction and caption translations by Alfred Werner. 209 illustrations. xxvii + 209pp. 9⅛ x 12¼.

21966-8 Paperbound $4.50

AGAINST THE GRAIN (A REBOURS), Joris K. Huysmans. Filled with weird images, evidences of a bizarre imagination, exotic experiments with hallucinatory drugs, rich tastes and smells and the diversions of its sybarite hero Duc Jean des Esseintes, this classic novel pushed 19th-century literary decadence to its limits. Full unabridged edition. Do not confuse this with abridged editions generally sold. Introduction by Havelock Ellis. xlix + 206pp.   22190-3 Paperbound $2.50

VARIORUM SHAKESPEARE: HAMLET. Edited by Horace H. Furness; a landmark of American scholarship. Exhaustive footnotes and appendices treat all doubtful words and phrases, as well as suggested critical emendations throughout the play's history. First volume contains editor's own text, collated with all Quartos and Folios. Second volume contains full first Quarto, translations of Shakespeare's sources (Belleforest, and Saxo Grammaticus), Der Bestrafte Brudermord, and many essays on critical and historical points of interest by major authorities of past and present. Includes details of staging and costuming over the years. By far the best edition available for serious students of Shakespeare. Total of xx + 905pp.
21004-9, 21005-7, 2 volumes, Paperbound $7.00

A LIFE OF WILLIAM SHAKESPEARE, Sir Sidney Lee. This is the standard life of Shakespeare, summarizing everything known about Shakespeare and his plays. Incredibly rich in material, broad in coverage, clear and judicious, it has served thousands as the best introduction to Shakespeare. 1931 edition. 9 plates. xxix + 792pp.   21967-4 Paperbound $4.50

MASTERS OF THE DRAMA, John Gassner. Most comprehensive history of the drama in print, covering every tradition from Greeks to modern Europe and America, including India, Far East, etc. Covers more than 800 dramatists, 2000 plays, with biographical material, plot summaries, theatre history, criticism, etc. "Best of its kind in English," New Republic. 77 illustrations. xxii + 890pp.
20100-7 Clothbound $10.00

THE EVOLUTION OF THE ENGLISH LANGUAGE, George McKnight. The growth of English, from the 14th century to the present. Unusual, non-technical account presents basic information in very interesting form: sound shifts, change in grammar and syntax, vocabulary growth, similar topics. Abundantly illustrated with quotations. Formerly Modern English in the Making. xii + 590pp.
21932-1 Paperbound $3.50

AN ETYMOLOGICAL DICTIONARY OF MODERN ENGLISH, Ernest Weekley. Fullest, richest work of its sort, by foremost British lexicographer. Detailed word histories, including many colloquial and archaic words; extensive quotations. Do not confuse this with the Concise Etymological Dictionary, which is much abridged. Total of xxvii + 830pp. 6½ x 9¼.
21873-2, 21874-0 Two volumes, Paperbound $7.90

FLATLAND: A ROMANCE OF MANY DIMENSIONS, E. A. Abbott. Classic of science-fiction explores ramifications of life in a two-dimensional world, and what happens when a three-dimensional being intrudes. Amusing reading, but also useful as introduction to thought about hyperspace. Introduction by Banesh Hoffmann. 16 illustrations. xx + 103pp.   20001-9 Paperbound $1.00

POEMS OF ANNE BRADSTREET, edited with an introduction by Robert Hutchinson. A new selection of poems by America's first poet and perhaps the first significant woman poet in the English language. 48 poems display her development in works of considerable variety—love poems, domestic poems, religious meditations, formal elegies, "quaternions," etc. Notes, bibliography. viii + 222pp.

22160-1 Paperbound $2.50

THREE GOTHIC NOVELS: THE CASTLE OF OTRANTO BY HORACE WALPOLE; VATHEK BY WILLIAM BECKFORD; THE VAMPYRE BY JOHN POLIDORI, WITH FRAGMENT OF A NOVEL BY LORD BYRON, edited by E. F. Bleiler. The first Gothic novel, by Walpole; the finest Oriental tale in English, by Beckford; powerful Romantic supernatural story in versions by Polidori and Byron. All extremely important in history of literature; all still exciting, packed with supernatural thrills, ghosts, haunted castles, magic, etc. xl + 291pp.

21232-7 Paperbound $3.00

THE BEST TALES OF HOFFMANN, E. T. A. Hoffmann. 10 of Hoffmann's most important stories, in modern re-editings of standard translations: Nutcracker and the King of Mice, Signor Formica, Automata, The Sandman, Rath Krespel, The Golden Flowerpot, Master Martin the Cooper, The Mines of Falun, The King's Betrothed, A New Year's Eve Adventure. 7 illustrations by Hoffmann. Edited by E. F. Bleiler. xxxix + 419pp.

21793-0 Paperbound $3.00

GHOST AND HORROR STORIES OF AMBROSE BIERCE, Ambrose Bierce. 23 strikingly modern stories of the horrors latent in the human mind: The Eyes of the Panther, The Damned Thing, An Occurrence at Owl Creek Bridge, An Inhabitant of Carcosa, etc., plus the dream-essay, Visions of the Night. Edited by E. F. Bleiler. xxii + 199pp.

20767-6 Paperbound $2.00

BEST GHOST STORIES OF J. S. LeFANU, J. Sheridan LeFanu. Finest stories by Victorian master often considered greatest supernatural writer of all. Carmilla, Green Tea, The Haunted Baronet, The Familiar, and 12 others. Most never before available in the U. S. A. Edited by E. F. Bleiler. 8 illustrations from Victorian publications. xvii + 467pp.

20415-4 Paperbound $3.00

MATHEMATICAL FOUNDATIONS OF INFORMATION THEORY, A. I. Khinchin. Comprehensive introduction to work of Shannon, McMillan, Feinstein and Khinchin, placing these investigations on a rigorous mathematical basis. Covers entropy concept in probability theory, uniqueness theorem, Shannon's inequality, ergodic sources, the E property, martingale concept, noise, Feinstein's fundamental lemma, Shanon's first and second theorems. Translated by R. A. Silverman and M. D. Friedman. iii + 120pp.

60434-9 Paperbound $2.00

SEVEN SCIENCE FICTION NOVELS, H. G. Wells. The standard collection of the great novels. Complete, unabridged. *First Men in the Moon, Island of Dr. Moreau, War of the Worlds, Food of the Gods, Invisible Man, Time Machine, In the Days of the Comet.* Not only science fiction fans, but every educated person owes it to himself to read these novels. 1015pp. (USO) 20264-X Clothbound $6.00

THE RED FAIRY BOOK, Andrew Lang. Lang's color fairy books have long been children's favorites. This volume includes Rapunzel, Jack and the Bean-stalk and 35 other stories, familiar and unfamiliar. 4 plates, 93 illustrations x + 367pp.
21673-X Paperbound $2.50

THE BLUE FAIRY BOOK, Andrew Lang. Lang's tales come from all countries and all times. Here are 37 tales from Grimm, the Arabian Nights, Greek Mythology, and other fascinating sources. 8 plates, 130 illustrations. xi + 390pp.
21437-0 Paperbound $2.75

HOUSEHOLD STORIES BY THE BROTHERS GRIMM. Classic English-language edition of the well-known tales — Rumpelstiltskin, Snow White, Hansel and Gretel, The Twelve Brothers, Faithful John, Rapunzel, Tom Thumb (52 stories in all). Translated into simple, straightforward English by Lucy Crane. Ornamented with headpieces, vignettes, elaborate decorative initials and a dozen full-page illustrations by Walter Crane. x + 269pp.
21080-4 Paperbound **$2.00**

THE MERRY ADVENTURES OF ROBIN HOOD, Howard Pyle. The finest modern versions of the traditional ballads and tales about the great English outlaw. Howard Pyle's complete prose version, with every word, every illustration of the first edition. Do not confuse this facsimile of the original (1883) with modern editions that change text or illustrations. 23 plates plus many page decorations. xxii + 296pp.
22043-5 Paperbound $2.75

THE STORY OF KING ARTHUR AND HIS KNIGHTS, Howard Pyle. The finest children's version of the life of King Arthur; brilliantly retold by Pyle, with 48 of his most imaginative illustrations. xviii + 313pp. 6⅛ x 9¼.
21445-1 Paperbound $2.50

THE WONDERFUL WIZARD OF OZ, L. Frank Baum. America's finest children's book in facsimile of first edition with all Denslow illustrations in full color. The edition a child should have. Introduction by Martin Gardner. 23 color plates, scores of drawings. iv + 267pp.
20691-2 Paperbound $3.50

THE MARVELOUS LAND OF OZ, L. Frank Baum. The second Oz book, every bit as imaginative as the Wizard. The hero is a boy named Tip, but the Scarecrow and the Tin Woodman are back, as is the Oz magic. 16 color plates, 120 drawings by John R. Neill. 287pp.
20692-0 Paperbound $2.50

THE MAGICAL MONARCH OF MO, L. Frank Baum. Remarkable adventures in a land even stranger than Oz. The best of Baum's books not in the Oz series. 15 color plates and dozens of drawings by Frank Verbeck. xviii + 237pp.
21892-9 Paperbound $2.25

THE BAD CHILD'S BOOK OF BEASTS, MORE BEASTS FOR WORSE CHILDREN, A MORAL ALPHABET, Hilaire Belloc. Three complete humor classics in one volume. Be kind to the frog, and do not call him names . . . and 28 other whimsical animals. Familiar favorites and some not so well known. Illustrated by Basil Blackwell. 156pp.
(USO) 20749-8 Paperbound $1.50

How to Know the Wild Flowers, Mrs. William Starr Dana. This is the classical book of American wildflowers (of the Eastern and Central United States), used by hundreds of thousands. Covers over 500 species, arranged in extremely easy to use color and season groups. Full descriptions, much plant lore. This Dover edition is the fullest ever compiled, with tables of nomenclature changes. 174 full-page plates by M. Satterlee. xii + 418pp. 20332-8 Paperbound $3.00

Our Plant Friends and Foes, William Atherton DuPuy. History, economic importance, essential botanical information and peculiarities of 25 common forms of plant life are provided in this book in an entertaining and charming style. Covers food plants (potatoes, apples, beans, wheat, almonds, bananas, etc.), flowers (lily, tulip, etc.), trees (pine, oak, elm, etc.), weeds, poisonous mushrooms and vines, gourds, citrus fruits, cotton, the cactus family, and much more. 108 illustrations. xiv + 290pp. 22272-1 Paperbound $2.50

How to Know the Ferns, Frances T. Parsons. Classic survey of Eastern and Central ferns, arranged according to clear, simple identification key. Excellent introduction to greatly neglected nature area. 57 illustrations and 42 plates. xvi + 215pp. 20740-4 Paperbound $2.00

Manual of the Trees of North America, Charles S. Sargent. America's foremost dendrologist provides the definitive coverage of North American trees and tree-like shrubs. 717 species fully described and illustrated: exact distribution, down to township; full botanical description; economic importance; description of subspecies and races; habitat, growth data; similar material. Necessary to every serious student of tree-life. Nomenclature revised to present. Over 100 locating keys. 783 illustrations. lii + 934pp. 20277-1, 20278-X Two volumes, Paperbound $7.00

Our Northern Shrubs, Harriet L. Keeler. Fine non-technical reference work identifying more than 225 important shrubs of Eastern and Central United States and Canada. Full text covering botanical description, habitat, plant lore, is paralleled with 205 full-page photographs of flowering or fruiting plants. Nomenclature revised by Edward G. Voss. One of few works concerned with shrubs. 205 plates, 35 drawings. xxviii + 521pp. 21989-5 Paperbound $3.75

The Mushroom Handbook, Louis C. C. Krieger. Still the best popular handbook: full descriptions of 259 species, cross references to another 200. Extremely thorough text enables you to identify, know all about any mushroom you are likely to meet in eastern and central U. S. A.: habitat, luminescence, poisonous qualities, use, folklore, etc. 32 color plates show over 50 mushrooms, also 126 other illustrations. Finding keys. vii + 560pp. 21861-9 Paperbound $4.50

Handbook of Birds of Eastern North America, Frank M. Chapman. Still much the best single-volume guide to the birds of Eastern and Central United States. Very full coverage of 675 species, with descriptions, life habits, distribution, similar data. All descriptions keyed to two-page color chart. With this single volume the average birdwatcher needs no other books. 1931 revised edition. 195 illustrations. xxxvi + 581pp. 21489-3 Paperbound $5.00

THE PHILOSOPHY OF THE UPANISHADS, Paul Deussen. Clear, detailed statement of upanishadic system of thought, generally considered among best available. History of these works, full exposition of system emergent from them, parallel concepts in the West. Translated by A. S. Geden. xiv + 429pp.

21616-0 Paperbound $3.50

LANGUAGE, TRUTH AND LOGIC, Alfred J. Ayer. Famous, remarkably clear introduction to the Vienna and Cambridge schools of Logical Positivism; function of philosophy, elimination of metaphysical thought, nature of analysis, similar topics. "Wish I had written it myself," Bertrand Russell. 2nd, 1946 edition. 160pp.

20010-8 Paperbound $1.50

THE GUIDE FOR THE PERPLEXED, Moses Maimonides. Great classic of medieval Judaism, major attempt to reconcile revealed religion (Pentateuch, commentaries) and Aristotelian philosophy. Enormously important in all Western thought. Unabridged Friedländer translation. 50-page introduction. lix + 414pp.

(USO) 20351-4 Paperbound $4.50

OCCULT AND SUPERNATURAL PHENOMENA, D. H. Rawcliffe. Full, serious study of the most persistent delusions of mankind: crystal gazing, mediumistic trance, stigmata, lycanthropy, fire walking, dowsing, telepathy, ghosts, ESP, etc., and their relation to common forms of abnormal psychology. Formerly *Illusions and Delusions of the Supernatural and the Occult.* iii + 551pp. 20503-7 Paperbound $4.00

THE EGYPTIAN BOOK OF THE DEAD: THE PAPYRUS OF ANI, E. A. Wallis Budge. Full hieroglyphic text, interlinear transliteration of sounds, word for word translation, then smooth, connected translation; Theban recension. Basic work in Ancient Egyptian civilization; now even more significant than ever for historical importance, dilation of consciousness, etc. clvi + 377pp. 6½ x 9¼.

21866-X Paperbound $4.95

PSYCHOLOGY OF MUSIC, Carl E. Seashore. Basic, thorough survey of everything known about psychology of music up to 1940's; essential reading for psychologists, musicologists. Physical acoustics; auditory apparatus; relationship of physical sound to perceived sound; role of the mind in sorting, altering, suppressing, creating sound sensations; musical learning, testing for ability, absolute pitch, other topics. Records of Caruso, Menuhin analyzed. 88 figures. xix + 408pp.

21851-1 Paperbound $3.50

THE I CHING (THE BOOK OF CHANGES), translated by James Legge. Complete translated text plus appendices by Confucius, of perhaps the most penetrating divination book ever compiled. Indispensable to all study of early Oriental civilizations. 3 plates. xxiii + 448pp. 21062-6 Paperbound $3.50

THE UPANISHADS, translated by Max Müller. Twelve classical upanishads: Chandogya, Kena, Aitareya, Kaushitaki, Isa, Katha, Mundaka, Taittiriyaka, Brhadaranyaka, Svetasvatara, Prasna, Maitriyana. 160-page introduction, analysis by Prof. Müller. Total of 670pp. 20992-X, 20993-8 Two volumes, Paperbound $7.50

INCIDENTS OF TRAVEL IN YUCATAN, John L. Stephens. Classic (1843) exploration of jungles of Yucatan, looking for evidences of Maya civilization. Stephens found many ruins; comments on travel adventures, Mexican and Indian culture. 127 striking illustrations by F. Catherwood. Total of 669 pp.
20926-1, 20927-X Two volumes, Paperbound $5.50

INCIDENTS OF TRAVEL IN CENTRAL AMERICA, CHIAPAS, AND YUCATAN, John L. Stephens. An exciting travel journal and an important classic of archeology. Narrative relates his almost single-handed discovery of the Mayan culture, and exploration of the ruined cities of Copan, Palenque, Utatlan and others; the monuments they dug from the earth, the temples buried in the jungle, the customs of poverty-stricken Indians living a stone's throw from the ruined palaces. 115 drawings by F. Catherwood. Portrait of Stephens. xii + 812pp.
22404-X, 22405-8 Two volumes, Paperbound $6.00

A NEW VOYAGE ROUND THE WORLD, William Dampier. Late 17-century naturalist joined the pirates of the Spanish Main to gather information; remarkably vivid account of buccaneers, pirates; detailed, accurate account of botany, zoology, ethnography of lands visited. Probably the most important early English voyage, enormous implications for British exploration, trade, colonial policy. Also most interesting reading. Argonaut edition, introduction by Sir Albert Gray. New introduction by Percy Adams. 6 plates, 7 illustrations. xlvii + 376pp. 6½ x 9¼.
21900-3 Paperbound $3.00

INTERNATIONAL AIRLINE PHRASE BOOK IN SIX LANGUAGES, Joseph W. Bátor. Important phrases and sentences in English paralleled with French, German, Portuguese, Italian, Spanish equivalents, covering all possible airport-travel situations; created for airline personnel as well as tourist by Language Chief, Pan American Airlines. xiv + 204pp.
22017-6 Paperbound $2.25

STAGE COACH AND TAVERN DAYS, Alice Morse Earle. Detailed, lively account of the early days of taverns; their uses and importance in the social, political and military life; furnishings and decorations; locations; food and drink; tavern signs, etc. Second half covers every aspect of early travel; the roads, coaches, drivers, etc. Nostalgic, charming, packed with fascinating material. 157 illustrations, mostly photographs. xiv + 449pp.
22518-6 Paperbound $4.00

NORSE DISCOVERIES AND EXPLORATIONS IN NORTH AMERICA, Hjalmar R. Holand. The perplexing Kensington Stone, found in Minnesota at the end of the 19th century. Is it a record of a Scandinavian expedition to North America in the 14th century? Or is it one of the most successful hoaxes in history. A scientific detective investigation. Formerly *Westward from Vinland*. 31 photographs, 17 figures. x + 354pp.
22014-1 Paperbound $2.75

A BOOK OF OLD MAPS, compiled and edited by Emerson D. Fite and Archibald Freeman. 74 old maps offer an unusual survey of the discovery, settlement and growth of America down to the close of the Revolutionary war: maps showing Norse settlements in Greenland, the explorations of Columbus, Verrazano, Cabot, Champlain, Joliet, Drake, Hudson, etc., campaigns of Revolutionary war battles, and much more. Each map is accompanied by a brief historical essay. xvi + 299pp. 11 x 13¾.
22084-2 Paperbound $7.00

MATHEMATICAL PUZZLES FOR BEGINNERS AND ENTHUSIASTS, Geoffrey Mott-Smith. 189 puzzles from easy to difficult—involving arithmetic, logic, algebra, properties of digits, probability, etc.—for enjoyment and mental stimulus. Explanation of mathematical principles behind the puzzles. 135 illustrations. viii + 248pp.
20198-8 Paperbound $2.00

PAPER FOLDING FOR BEGINNERS, William D. Murray and Francis J. Rigney. Easiest book on the market, clearest instructions on making interesting, beautiful origami. Sail boats, cups, roosters, frogs that move legs, bonbon boxes, standing birds, etc. 40 projects; more than 275 diagrams and photographs. 94pp.
20713-7 Paperbound $1.00

TRICKS AND GAMES ON THE POOL TABLE, Fred Herrmann. 79 tricks and games— some solitaires, some for two or more players, some competitive games—to entertain you between formal games. Mystifying shots and throws, unusual caroms, tricks involving such props as cork, coins, a hat, etc. Formerly *Fun on the Pool Table*. 77 figures. 95pp.
21814-7 Paperbound $1.25

HAND SHADOWS TO BE THROWN UPON THE WALL: A SERIES OF NOVEL AND AMUSING FIGURES FORMED BY THE HAND, Henry Bursill. Delightful picturebook from great-grandfather's day shows how to make 18 different hand shadows: a bird that flies, duck that quacks, dog that wags his tail, camel, goose, deer, boy, turtle, etc. Only book of its sort. vi + 33pp. 6½ x 9¼. 21779-5 Paperbound $1.00

WHITTLING AND WOODCARVING, E. J. Tangerman. 18th printing of best book on market. "If you can cut a potato you can carve" toys and puzzles, chains, chessmen, caricatures, masks, frames, woodcut blocks, surface patterns, much more. Information on tools, woods, techniques. Also goes into serious wood sculpture from Middle Ages to present, East and West. 464 photos, figures. x + 293pp.
20965-2 Paperbound $2.50

HISTORY OF PHILOSOPHY, Julián Marías. Possibly the clearest, most easily followed, best planned, most useful one-volume history of philosophy on the market; neither skimpy nor overfull. Full details on system of every major philosopher and dozens of less important thinkers from pre-Socratics up to Existentialism and later. Strong on many European figures usually omitted. Has gone through dozens of editions in Europe. 1966 edition, translated by Stanley Appelbaum and Clarence Strowbridge. xviii + 505pp.
21739-6 Paperbound $3.50

YOGA: A SCIENTIFIC EVALUATION, Kovoor T. Behanan. Scientific but non-technical study of physiological results of yoga exercises; done under auspices of Yale U. Relations to Indian thought, to psychoanalysis, etc. 16 photos. xxiii + 270pp.
20505-3 Paperbound $2.50

Prices subject to change without notice.
Available at your book dealer or write for free catalogue to Dept. GI, Dover Publications, Inc., 180 Varick St., N. Y., N. Y. 10014. Dover publishes more than 150 books each year on science, elementary and advanced mathematics, biology, music, art, literary history, social sciences and other areas.